Pete&Pickles

The Indepen-dent Pig

Berkeley Breathed

PHILOMEL BOOKS

For Sophie & Milo

P
ete was a perfectly predictable pig.

He was also a perfectly practical pig.
And a perfectly uncomplicated pig.

Being all those perfect things, Pete might have run for the hills if he had known what was coming that night.

The storm arrived first. Pete cut the evening's fun off early and went to bed to get the nightmare out of the way—the same terrifying watery nightmare all pigs dream during stormy nights. For pigs are known for doing only one thing well in water:

Drowning.

And that is exactly what Pete dreamt he was doing when a sudden sound woke him.

The window was open. Pete pulled the lamp switch. Nothing happened.

He had an odd feeling—pigs are very smart in this way—that something was a little . . .

wrong.

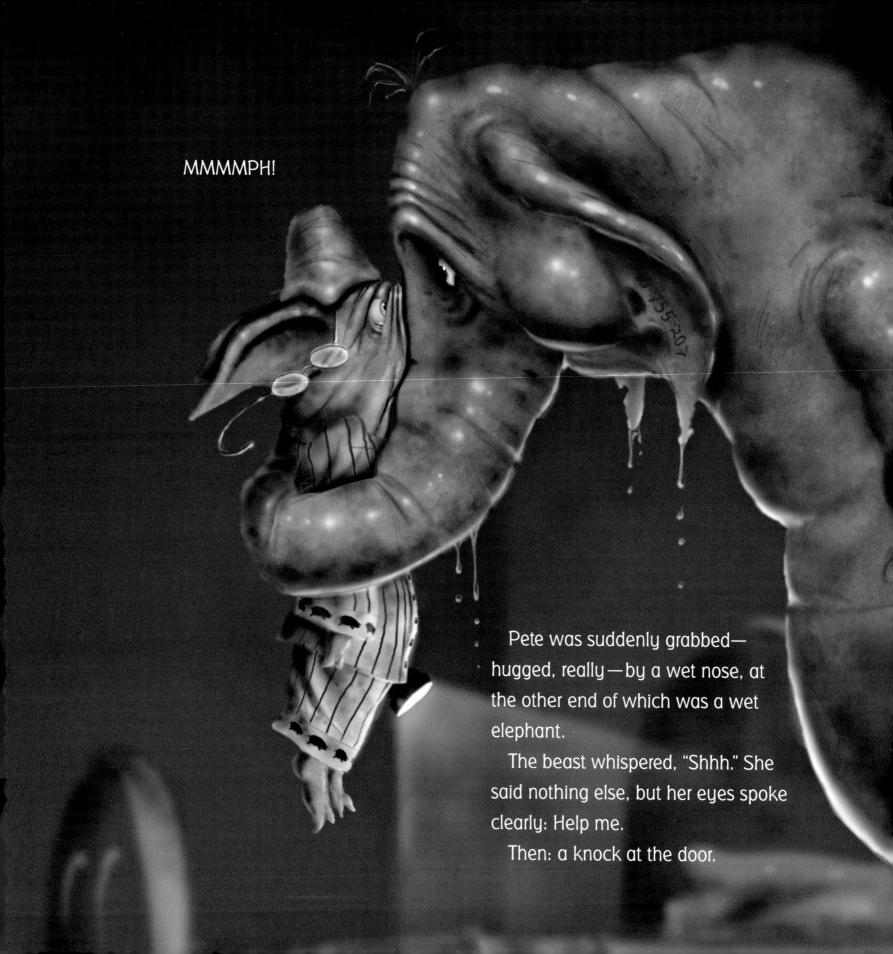

MMMMPH!

Pete was suddenly grabbed—
hugged, really—by a wet nose, at
the other end of which was a wet
elephant.

The beast whispered, "Shhh." She
said nothing else, but her eyes spoke
clearly: Help me.

Then: a knock at the door.

A clown asked Pete if he'd seen any sign of an escaped elephant named Pickles.

"THERE! Under the couch! Look carefully!" Pete said.

As the circus man led the sad, slumping elephant away, Pete was startled when she looked back at him . . . and smiled.

The next morning, Pete was disinfecting his house
when he noticed his midnight visitor had left behind
a gift. Dandelions.

Ridiculous, thought Pete as he scrubbed.

That afternoon, Pete took his usual short stroll. He
looked down at the evening mist rolling in and saw
a circus tent. He looked at the dandelion. "Ridiculous,"
he muttered.

Today, however, Pete would take a longer walk.

He soon found himself amidst the circus tents, watching
a long nose plucking every dandelion within reach.

Pete knew that nose.

And it knew *him*. It plucked Pete's hat and disappeared.

Seconds before Pete called the police, his hat was pushed back out.

Improved.

Pete looked in to see Pickles sitting
in a very dark corner of a very dark tent
wearing a very locked chain.

Pete suddenly, unexplainably, found
himself reaching for the key.

Now free and outside, Pickles dove to hide while a panicked Pete whispered, "TEA was on my schedule today! NOT elephants!"

Being a practical pig, however, he knew they needed a disguise. Something! Anything! Pete thought fast . . .

It worked! Too well! A policeman suggested dinner.

They reached Pete's house by nightfall. A weary Pickles
retired after making herself comfortable in a pair of Pete's
favorite pajamas.

Understand this: you have not heard snoring until you
have had an elephant nap on your couch. Pete was a
perfectly unpleased pig.

Tomorrow, he thought, *the big girl leaves*.

Pete awoke the next day to find Pickles doing a little morning
tai chi . . . as if she were in China.
Which she certainly was not.

On the other hand, Pete noted that his houseguest had made a few changes to the grounds. This time Pete did NOT say "ridiculous."

Later that morning, Pete experienced the goosebumpily joy of a back scrubbing with his newspaper and coffee.

He also discovered the limits of his bathtub.

Pickles showed Pete a magazine article about high-diving. She pointed to both of them.

"Ridiculous," Pete said. "Pigs and elephants sink like bricks."

Pickles smiled. After lunch they would swan-dive off Niagara Falls.

And they did. Sort of.

On Tuesday, they sledded down the Matterhorn in Switzerland. Sort of.

Pete was learning that Pickles had *lots* of plans.

On Sunday, they went to Tahiti for brunch.
Pickles, as always, shared her tropical refreshment
with the natives.

After Paris, it was on to the lazy canals of Venice. Pete did not know any romantic Italian songs, which did not stop him from singing them.

Pickles sniffed a fragrant Venetian lily and shared it with Pete in a manner nicely suited for elephants and pigs.

It was when Pete returned home one evening and found ballet tryouts in Moscow, soaring para-cows over Tuscany and housepainters on his roof that his thoughts turned to his earlier life.

A less complicated life, thought Pete.

Soon after, Pete discovered
Pickles getting into things
she shouldn't have been in.
He snapped.

Paprika

"I am a predictable, practical, uncomplicated pig! Or I was BEFORE!" he yelled.

As a shocked Pickles fell back into the bathtub, the last words she remembered hearing were the worst:

"IT'S TIME YOU PROBABLY LEFT!"

Paprika

Something broke! A pipe gushed water in a
spewing torrent! The house filled while a panicky
Pete screamed, "Pickles!
The mop!
Buckets!
Sponges!
Never mind!

HEAD UP FOR HIGH GROUND!"

Pete worried that the high ground would run out. And as a matter of fact . . .

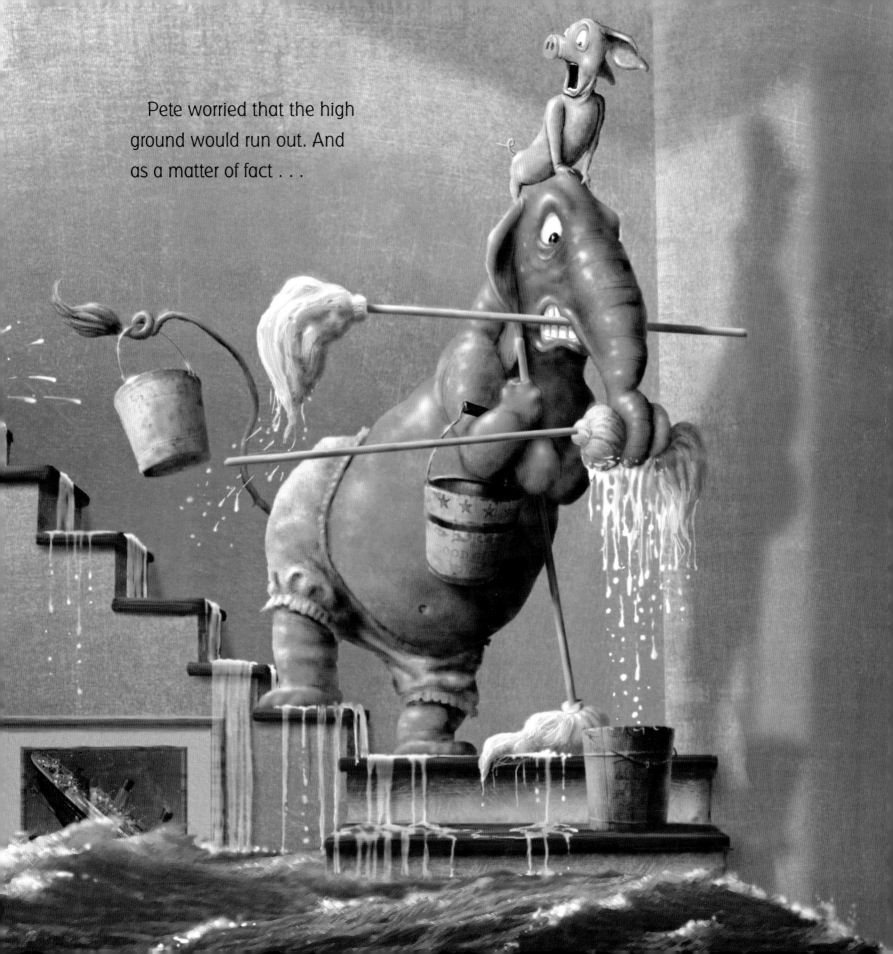

. . . it did.

And when all the snouts and snoots in the now flooded house were fully stretched to their furthest reach . . . only one had found the refuge of sweet air.

Pete clung tightly to the last open
window. He looked back down into the
face of one far too heavy to join him . . .
and noticed, once again, as always . . .

. . . a smile.

At that terrible moment, what occurred to Pete was NOT how his life had become so unpredictable, so unpractical . . . and so completely complicated with Pickles.

No, what occurred to Pete was his life without her.

That endless night would be the longest of all their great journeys. And when the fireman finally climbed to the window the next morning, he could not believe what he found.

He found a very small pig breathing for a very large elephant.
All night. Every hour. Every minute. Every breath shared.

When they finally emptied the house, the firemen looked down
in puzzlement at the exhausted pair of sleeping friends. They tried
but could not pull Pete from the mighty grasp of Pickles.

The two slept all day, through the night and on until morning . . .

. . . when they awoke to pick blueberries
on the Dandelion Moons of Pluto.

Pete sang Italian love songs.

PHILOMEL BOOKS A division of Penguin Young Readers Group. Published by The Penguin Group. Penguin Group (USA) Inc., 375 Hudson Street, New York, NY 10014, U.S.A. Penguin Group (Canada), 90 Eglinton Avenue East, Suite 700, Toronto, Ontario M4P 2Y3, Canada (a division of Pearson Penguin Canada Inc.). Penguin Books Ltd, 80 Strand, London WC2R 0RL, England. Penguin Ireland, 25 St. Stephen's Green, Dublin 2, Ireland (a division of Penguin Books Ltd). Penguin Group (Australia), 250 Camberwell Road, Camberwell, Victoria 3124, Australia (a division of Pearson Australia Group Pty Ltd). Penguin Books India Pvt Ltd, 11 Community Centre, Panchsheel Park, New Delhi - 110 017, India. Penguin Group (NZ), 67 Apollo Drive, Rosedale, North Shore 0632, New Zealand (a division of Pearson New Zealand Ltd). Penguin Books (South Africa) (Pty) Ltd, 24 Sturdee Avenue, Rosebank, Johannesburg 2196, South Africa. Penguin Books Ltd, Registered Offices: 80 Strand, London WC2R 0RL, England.
Published simultaneously in Canada. Manufactured in China by South China Printing Co. Ltd. Design by Richard Amari. Text set in Badger Light. The illustrations were created with virtual acrylics and virtual watercolor on 100% rag archival virtual illustration board.
Library of Congress Cataloging-in-Publication Data is available upon request.
ISBN 978-0-399-25082-8 10 9 8 7 6 5 4